WITCHES

BOOK ONE

Episodes
One thru Four

by J. Smith Kirkland

Introduction

Witches is a tale about modern day witches derived from legends and told in soap opera format.

Witches: Book One is composed of four episodes, each released as a separate ebook, and published together in paperback as "Book One".

Episode One: "A Bad Spell" introduces the cast in this melodrama, especially Jack: a mortal who falls into the hidden world of witches, or maybe is pushed into it when his brother Aron goes missing.

Episode Two: "Finding Aron" follows Jack as he navigates through the strange witch world to find Aron. At times, he is convinced it is all just a bad dream, but he will do whatever it takes to find his brother.

Episode Three: "Stone Cold" brings a visitor from an ancient legend to visit the world of Witches. And he brings vengeance with him. Aron finds himself needing the witches' help again, and Jack finds the witches need his help this time.

Episode Four: "Vodou" finds another stranger in town. She has more than one purpose for coming here, but the players in this book seem to attract those who deal in revenge. She has her eye on Aron, and she is not one to be denied what she wants.

Table of Contents

Episode One

A BAD SPELL

A Bad Spell

Aron feels a hot breath on the back of his neck. It reeks like rotted meat between teeth. His heart races while he runs as fast as his legs can move, but it keeps closing in on him. Whatever it is makes a raspy growl that is half hunger half laughter. Aron keeps trying to look behind him to see how close it is, but he stumbles on a curb and falls into the street. He expects to be devoured before he can get back on his feet, but he bounces back up quickly. He sees nothing. Before he has time to feel relief, he feels the heat and the stench of the heavy breath again.

§

Meanwhile, in her cozy suburban home, Sunder stands at the kitchen table working over a large black kettle of steaming liquid with bits of twigs and leaves floating in it. Her mother's cookbook on the table is open to a recipe called "Blackened Swan." Sunder waves a gemstone necklace over the swirling grume. She glances at the cook book and smiles. This recipe is so much more fun without her mother scrutinizing her the entire time.

"You can't hide from me, Aron."

As she enjoys beshrewing poor Aron, she is startled from her brew by the sound of the front door flying open. She hears Jack's voice in the living room.

"Sunder!"

She can't let Jack see what she is doing. No one can know, but especially not Jack. He would never understand that she is doing this for him. Her mind races. She has to stop him from coming into the kitchen. In her panic, she loses her hold on the necklace, and it drops into the kettle, disappearing in the mix. This can't be good, but no time to fish it out. She rushes for the living room, pulling the curtain in the kitchen doorway closed. She quickly blocks Jack before he can see what she has going on in there.

"Sunder. Sunder, Aron is missing. Nobody's heard from him since yesterday."

Sunder gently moves Jack farther back into the living room, away from the kitchen. She knows how to use her voice to soothe people, and often uses it better than any magic she knows. She speaks to him like a yogi giving instructions to a class.

"Calm down. Take a breath. Start over. What are you talking about?"

As she attempts to console Jack, she is also trying to convince herself to stay calm. She looks back towards the kitchen. She has screwed up spells before. It's never good. She needs to get back in there and assess the damage, but she needs to get Jack under control first.

"No one can find Aron. He was supposed to meet me to pick up the rings this morning, and he didn't show."

"Maybe there was something else he had to do. Maybe he forgot."

"He wouldn't have forgotten to pick up the rings; the wedding is tomorrow."

"Maybe he got cold feet."

"My brother is an idiot sometimes, but he knows Jenna is the best thing that ever happened to him. He didn't get cold feet. His car is at home, and no one can find him."

Sunder has to figure out a way to be there for Jack, and still get him out of her house so she can triage whatever injury the interruption to her potion caused. She gets a minute to think when Jack's phone rings.

"Jenna, did you find him?...No...okay...I'm going to go back to the jeweler's...okay...okay."

Jack ends the call and gives Sunder a quick hug.

"I have to go."

This works, she thinks. She can offer to help, but Jack will have to leave. And whatever has happened to Aron just means Jack is going to have to stay in town longer than he had planned. That's just more time to find a way to make Jack realize how much he loves her. It's perfect.

"Why don't you stay here and just relax for a minute? I'll make you some tea. I'm sure he'll show up with some funny story about where he's been."

"I sure hope so. If you hear from him, tell him he's in big trouble."

"Jack, sit down for a minute."

"No, I have to go back to the jeweler's to get the rings before they close. I'll call you."

Jack leaves on the same whirlwind that brought him into the house. Sunder locks the door behind him, then returns quickly to the kitchen. She stands over the kettle, looking at it like it is a burnt Thanksgiving turkey.

"Hmmm...a little over-cooked."

She frantically pours out the potion onto a kitchen towel in the sink to search for the necklace, but it's gone. How can it be gone? She picks up her mother's cookbook and starts reading the recipe to see if it says anything about how to uncook the spell. Of course not; Mother never made mistakes.

"I hate cooking."

§

Aron is still running through the downtown streets. His jeans and shirt are muddy and torn. Most people pretend not to notice him as he pushes past them while looking back in terror at something they cannot see. Just another crazy homeless guy. He thinks he is being chased. Obviously insane. Still, they look back, just to make sure nothing is there.

He turns down an alley. Dead end. But the breath has stopped. Aron can't hear the growling. Maybe he outran it. Maybe he lost it. Heart still racing, he stops about halfway down the alley and looks back. Nothing there. It's gone. He tries to catch his breath. Then a crash behind him. He spins around. Nothing, just a fallen garbage can. Probably a cat. But on the back of his neck and up his nostrils, that warm, rotted breath. He feels dizzy, like he's falling, like he's fading. Dissolving.

The Sweet Woman

Jack tries to get hold of Aron on his cell phone as he goes to the jewelry store. Jenna calls again.

"No, I haven't heard from him either, but I'm about to pick up the rings."

He stops and looks at the building next to him.

"What was the address of the jeweler's?"

Jack looks around at the stores nearby. No jeweler's. He pulls a business card from his pocket.

"Yeah that's what I had, too. I think it may be wrong. Okay. Call me if you hear anything."

The address is on the business card. He was just there this morning. This has to be where it was. This building should be the jeweler's, but instead it's a dessert place called The Sweet Woman's Shoppe.

Maybe he's on the wrong Market Street. Maybe it's like Atlanta where there are 30 different Peachtree Streets. He googles the jeweler's name on his phone. Same address. The website has an ad for a sale this week, so not old info. He tries to use the GPS, but it just keeps showing the little "thinking" image. He looks at the street sign on the corner, the number over the door of the sweet shop, the business card. Doesn't make sense. This has to be where he was before. Maybe his brain is just scrambled from the stress. Maybe that's what happened to Aron. Maybe he is lost downtown somewhere looking for this evasive jeweler.

Jack goes into the sweet shop to ask directions. He looks

around the shop. No one else there. He is about to leave when he notices a woman behind the counter. She was somehow camouflaged against the display of cakes and sweets. She is your basic Betty Crocker, home cooking, mom type. A 1950s style dress, flowery apron with ruffles, pearls, and heels. Her hair is one of those styles that could be described as "she had her hair done yesterday." It has just the right amount of flip in the back and one immovable curl casually placed off center on her forehead to perfectly frame her face. She is dusting flour off the front of her apron. She doesn't seem to care that her left cheek is also dusted with flour, and there is some in her hair.

"Excuse me, I think I got lost while I was talking on my phone. I'm looking for a jeweler's store."

"Jeweler . . . hmmm . . . on this street?"

"I thought so, but . . ."

"Let me look on the Internet."

Before Jack can explain that he did that already, she continues.

"Why don't you have a sweet while I look it up. On the house, of course."

She studies him for a few seconds as if to determine exactly what type of alien he is. Then with a quick smile and the flick of a wrist, she offers him a small plate of petit fours.

"Here, I think you'll like this one."

Jack cautiously takes one of the sweets from the plate. She turns and walks away from the counter, disappearing into a back room.

"Thank you," Jack calls back to her.

It does look good. He loves that overly sweet white candy icing they put on petit fours. It's like a tiny wedding cake. And the little rosebud splat of soft sugary icing on top is just enough. Maybe Jenna will have these at the reception.

As he enjoys the little dessert, he turns to look around the place and sees a man sitting at one of the tables. On the table is a half-eaten piece of lemon meringue pie and a glass of milk. Jack is certain the man and his odd meal were not there before.

"Delicious desserts. Would you like to sit?"

"No thanks; I'm in a hurry."

The man is dressed in distinguished yet eccentric clothes. His suit coat is classic, maybe from the 1800s, but somewhat oversized. His shirt is a simple dress shirt in a surprising shade of purple, and his silver glasses are round wire frames surrounding pale rose-tinted lenses. Jack doesn't realize he is staring at the man so intently until he is startled as the man speaks again.

"You know, sometimes we don't recognize what we are looking for when we find it."

"I'm sorry."

"For what?"

"No. I mean, I didn't understand what you said."

"Oh. Just that things aren't always what they appear to be, and sometimes we doubt what we should trust, and we trust what we should doubt."

"Uh huh."

Jack turns back to the counter to look for the woman.

"Look, I have to leave. Can you tell her thanks for me?"

When he turns back the man is gone, along with his plate. Actually, there's no sign he was ever there. No pie, no plate, no glass, no man. Jack even peeks under the table, as if the man may be trying to hide. Nothing. Jack looks back at the counter. The woman is there holding a piece of paper out to Jack. He checks to make sure the man is still gone, and then that the woman is still back.

"Where did he go?"

"I'm sorry, love, where did who go?"

"The man that was at that table."

"What man?"

She doesn't really give Jack time to answer that.

"Here's the address of the jeweler's. I think you'll find it's not far at all."

Jack takes the paper, and thanks her for the directions and the cake. As he leaves the shop, he tries to put away thoughts of the bizarreness of this place in order to return his attention to the task at hand.

The Sweet Woman smiles as the door closes. "My pleasure, Jack."

Outside the shop, Jack takes out his cell phone to call Jenna. He looks back at the sweet shop door, but it's not there. It's the jeweler's. Jack looks at the other storefronts around him. No sweet shop. He checks the address on the paper the woman gave him. It's the same as the business card. He checks again that he is now standing at that address, in front of the jeweler's. The same one he was at this morning.

"I'm losing my mind."

The Cat

Sunder paces in front of an open window in her living room. The curtains dance in the wind. She has spread tarot cards over a Ouija board on the coffee table. It has been hours since the accident with the potion, and Sunder is starting to worry that the damage cannot be undone.

Looking out the window as if someone is there, she says, "You should at least be here by now. This can't be happening."

Whatever happened to Aron, he should be trying to find his way back to her; her mother's notes say the victim of this spell always returns to the source. Victim. Such a negative word. Her mother always was the 'glass half-empty" kind. The recipient. The recipient of the spell. That sounds much better to Sunder.

As she focuses on making what she does sound as benevolent as she imagines it to be, Sunder hears a noise outside. An orange tabby cat sits in the window. The missing necklace hangs around its neck.

"There you are."

She picks up the cat and carefully removes the necklace. She puts it around her own neck.

"This is not what I had planned, but we'll just have to make it work."

Jenna

Jenna sits at her kitchen table with a cup of coffee. That's the only thing she has felt like having all day. Though she did think that this might be a good day to take up drinking. The day before her wedding and her fiancé is missing. That seems like a good trigger for a drinking problem.

Her cell phone and laptop are in front of her so she can respond quickly to any call, text, or email. Browser tabs filled with searches for how to locate missing persons. Jack paces with nervous energy back and forth across the kitchen. He is not making her less tense.

"We'll find him, Jenna. The police say we can file a missing persons report, but they won't be looking very hard after one day without any evidence of a struggle or something. They say come back tomorrow because they still think he'll show up, but I'm going to make some flyers to put up around town."

"What if he doesn't want us to find him?"

"Jenna, he didn't leave you. He wouldn't. Something had to have happened."

"I don't know which one scares me more."

Selanya

Armed with his stack of neon yellow papers, rolls of tape, and a stapler, Jack is on his mission to put 'missing' flyers in every shop window and on every utility pole. He goes into a bookstore to see if they will let him post a sign there.

There is a woman behind the counter. In his rush, Jack almost doesn't notice how strikingly attractive she is. Almost. She's dressed in modernized '70s clothes, a very stylish hippie look. Her hair beckons for a chain of daisies to wear. Jack always looks business-meeting-ready because he usually has to for work, but inside he has always felt a little bit hippie. He suddenly feels out of place and unprepared with his dress pants and stiff shirt. At least he didn't put on a tie this morning.

"Hi, do you mind if I put a missing person flyer in your window?"

"Please do."

Jack turns back towards the door, prepping his tape dispenser.

"May I see one?"

"Of course. Thank you. Have you seen him?"

Jack goes back to the woman and hands her a flyer. She looks at it and doesn't hesitate to respond.

"Yes. Actually, I have. He bought a book here last week."

"Really? Have you seen him since yesterday?"

"No, I'm sorry."

"Well, thanks for letting me post a flyer. And if you do see him . . ."

As he is talking to her, he notices a plate of sweets on the counter. The same type of petit fours he had in the disappearing sweet shop.

"Where did you get those?"

"A good friend of mine has a sweet shop."

"On Market Street?"

She looks at him as if she is puzzled, or maybe suspicious.

"You've been there?"

"Yes. Well. No."

Jack is not really sure how to answer this question. He sort of wanted to forget that happened. He half-believed it didn't. What could he say that wouldn't make her think he was crazy, or make himself think he was crazy?

"I'm not really sure."

"So you have been there."

"And you go there?"

"When I can."

"You mean when it's there?"

"You have definitely been there."

Jack is a little relieved, and a little disturbed, that someone else knows about the place.

"So I'm not crazy? I was thinking maybe the cryptic man was my other personality or something."

"Cryptic man?"

She studies Jack for a minute, as he tries to think how he can unsay what he just said.

"You met Shamus," she says, "at the Sweet Shop."

Jack shrugs his shoulders. She looks away, and Jack thinks she just had that same feeling that she should not have said the words out loud.

"I didn't catch his name."

She walks from behind the counter and motions for Jack to move to a comfy chair sitting area over by the bookshelves.

"I'm Selanya. I think maybe we should talk. Tell me some more about your brother."

"How did you know it was my brother?"

"Didn't you say that?"

"No."

"Well, I can see there is a strong family resemblance from the picture."

Selanya is just beautiful enough for Jack to accept that explanation without further question.

He Will Stay

"He'll show up before tomorrow," Sunder says to Jenna.

"I'm not sure, Sunder."

They sit sipping cups of tea at Jenna's kitchen table. Sunder has come by Jenna's under the guise of consoling her. But mainly she wants to extract anything Jenna knows about what Jack is doing and thinking. She watches as Jenna stacks and re-stacks sugar packets on the table and moves the napkin holder and salt and pepper so they align in different patterns. Jenna is wearing her usual T-shirt and jeans, but the shirt is wrinkled like she slept in it. She has either not combed her hair today, or she has fretted her hands through it enough to make it look like bedhead.

Sunder on the other hand is camera-ready as usual with her trademark pink-accented outfit. She really wants to have Jenna go find a brush, but knows she has to stay in the worried friend role instead.

"I'll do whatever I can to help find him. And I'm so glad Jack is here for you right now."

"I know. He's been a rock. I think I would have just crumbled without him around."

"It's too bad he lives so far away now."

"Oh, he says he'll stay here until we find Aron. He can work remotely for a while."

"That's good." Sunder says, turning to look out the

window. "That's very good," she whispers to herself. It gives her more time to make Jack realize he is in love with her.

Jenna checks her phone. No calls.

"I just don't know what to think. We've called all the hospitals. I think he may have changed his mind."

Sunder tries to return her focus to Jenna. Poor Jenna. She has always appeared so strong and independent. But right now, it looks as if Jenna may break into pieces over something as minute as being left at the altar. If Sunder's fiancé were missing, she wouldn't be sitting around thinking up scenarios for why he left; she would be hunting him down. But oh yeah, Jenna.

"Jenna, I am sure Aron loves you."

"I know he loves me, but maybe he's just not ready to commit to that love."

"It's true, sometimes men need a little help realizing they are ready for that. But Jack will come around. I mean Aron. Aron will show up soon."

It's not like Sunder to misspeak. She looks at Jenna suspiciously and thinks to herself, "What is in this tea?"

But she dismisses any thought of intent on Jenna's part; Jenna is so sickeningly caring and compassionate, which is exactly why she is so easy to manipulate.

She's a Witch

Selanya hands Jack a black book. There is no writing or marking of any kind on the cover.

"Your brother bought a copy of this book. He was asking how to find out if someone is a witch."

"A witch? He was looking for a witch?"

Selanya smiles.

"He found a witch. He wanted to know if he already knew another one or not."

"So you're a witch?"

"I practice a little magic."

Jack is not sure if she is toying with him or not. He wouldn't mind if she was being flirtatious.

"Like *Charmed* or *Bewitched*?"

"More like *Dark Shadows* or *Practical Magic*."

"And the cryptic man? He's also a witch or warlock or whatever?"

Selanya seems more serious at the mention of Shamus.

"Shamus is a special kind of witch. They say his soul can travel between the three spheres, and through time."

"So, staying with the TV/movie theme; he's sorta like Doctor Who?"

"That's as good a description as any I guess. He is a doctor of sorts, but maybe with a little Doctor Bombay mixed in for good measure."

Jack is enjoying this game, but he remembers he has more important things to attend to.

"What does all this have to do with my brother?"

"Your brother was in here trying to find out how to tell if someone is a witch. He suspected someone. Then he disappears. Then Shamus shows up and talks to you. Shamus doesn't do anything randomly. I think a witch may have something to do with your brother's disappearance."

Jack suddenly feels like she is taking the game too far. His brother is missing, and she is about to cross that line on the chart of crazy vs. attraction in the wrong direction.

"OK, this has been fun, but I have to go look for my brother."

Jack hands Selanya the book, gathers his supplies, and turns to go. He only stops at the door long enough to tape a flyer to the glass. He doesn't look back to see Selanya's look of concern.

Aron

As Jack leaves Selanya's shop, he continues down the street looking for more places to put flyers. He isn't sure the flyers will help at all, but it keeps him from feeling completely helpless. He is not used to being helpless.

A sudden gust of wind snatches half the flyers from his hand and throws them down the sidewalk. Jack chases after, catching most of them, but some whirl into an alley. He bends down to grab the last one as it slides to a stop. When he stands, he sees a figure silhouetted at the other end of the alley. The figure turns so the light catches his face.

"Aron!"

Jack runs towards him, but Aron runs out the other end of the alley and takes off down the street. Jack chases after him across the street, around a corner, and across another street. He calls out to Aron, but Aron keeps running, looking behind him like someone besides Jack is chasing him. Someone, or something. Something horrible.

Jack is gaining on him when Aron runs into an empty parking deck. He runs in after Aron, but slows to a stop as he looks around and realizes Aron is not there. There was no way he could have made it across the parking deck before Jack came in, but he isn't there. It was like he vanished into thin air.

An alley cat hisses as it slinks out of the shadows startling Jack. The cat runs past him and out of the deck.

OK, I Get It

Selanya opens a box of new books that were delivered earlier. She loves the smell of new press as much as the musty smell of the old books.

The shop door flies open. She looks up to see Jack standing in the doorway, bent over with his hands on his knees, out of breath.

He puffs out his words, "I think I've gone crazy, but something strange is going on. Can you teach me any of that magic that will help me find my brother?"

Episode Two

A New Witch in Town

Sunder arrives downtown for an art opening at the gallery. She can't really do much about the Aron situation right now. The cat got out somehow, but it will come back. She's just going to have to let the spell work itself out, and it's very important to admire art; people admire you when you admire art. She doesn't really care for graphic art but this new artist was the topic of conversation at the wine tastings last week.

Dressed for the occasion, and wearing her nighttime sunglasses for effect, she can't wait to socialize with the artistic crowd. But as she starts down the sidewalk towards the gallery, she sees Jack leaving the bookstore. Sunder knows a woman owns that shop. A very attractive woman. She moves to the shadow between the store lights and watches as Jack leaves.

He doesn't see her as he heads down the sidewalk away from her. Once he is far enough away, Sunder approaches the shop and looks in the window. She sees Selanya walking towards the bookshelves. Selanya reaches her hand out towards the shelves and a book slides out into her hand.

Sunder moves away from the window and back into the shadows. How unexpected that she would find a witch in town that she wasn't aware of already. She grasps the amulet on her necklace and rubs it between her fingers.

Sunder thinks, *She's not just some midtown shopkeeper; is she? No, she's something more than that.*

She watches as Selanya thumbs through the book looking for something specific. Maybe a love potion, Sunder thinks.

And she's trying to take Jack from me. Something tells me I need to meet this witch.

Learning the Craft

On the eve of her wedding, if there is a wedding tomorrow, Jenna sits at her kitchen table as her future brother-in-law chattily paces around the room. Jack's telling her all about meeting Selanya and what she's teaching him. Jenna is skeptical. And worried that Selanya is taking advantage of him somehow.

"I'm not much for this magic stuff. Sometimes I think you trust what you should doubt, Jack."

"What?"

"I'm just saying, I'm not sure I would trust her."

"No. I just, someone else said that same thing to me. The man in the sweets shop."

"The disappearing man?"

"I know, I think I'm losing it, too. I'm not sure what I'm doing anymore. Everything seems like a dream, I just want to know what happened to Aron."

Jenna gets up from the table and stops Jack from pacing.

"Look at me. I don't know what's going on, Jack. I don't think you're crazy, but something is definitely not normal here, and it scares me a little. Just be careful."

Jenna walks out of the room. Jack watches her leave, and then notices the mirror in the hall as she passes it. Maybe he should try the locating spell that Selanya taught him. It uses a mirror. Jack walks over and looks at his reflection. Who is that guy staring back?

"Jack, you have completely lost it. Witches. Spells. Disappearing places. And people. Well, if you're going to go mad, might as well jump in feet first. Let's give this location spell thing a try."

Jack stares into the mirror. Imagining he is Aron looking at the reflection of Jack. Pretending he is looking into his own eyes from the eyes of Aron.

"This is crazy."

He looks away from the mirror. Spells are not real. Witches are not real. But something is wrong with his brother. He has to find a way to help Aron. A way to find Aron.

"Come on, just try it. Concentrate."

He takes a deep breath and stares into the eyes of his reflection. He forgets everything around him and just imagines that Aron can somehow see him, that they are connected. His vision starts to tunnel so all he sees is his own face. Then everything fades and changes.

Jack sees Sunder in the reflection. She is talking with a cat. The cat he saw in the parking deck. He sees her taking a necklace from around the cat's neck. Then, like waking too fast from a dream, he is back and staring at his own drop-jawed reflection. He's not sure what just happened, or what it means, but Jenna may be right; something is definitely not normal.

Welcome to My World

A new day, and since it looks like Aron won't "return" in time for the wedding, Sunder has time to check out her new competition. She pretends to be shopping as she monitors Selanya when she's not looking, but Selanya notices her standing at the jewelry display for quite some time. Too long to just be looking at jewelry.

"Hi. Can I help you find anything?"

"I'm just checking out the store. I haven't been in here before."

"Well, I'm glad you stopped by. I'm Selanya."

"Sunder Bouchard."

Sunder likes to use her family name in introductions. It adds a bit of prestige to let people know from the very beginning that she demands respect. Selanya extends her hand. And after a slight hesitation, Sunder accepts it. As their hands touch Selanya gets a flash of insight.

§

Sunder is making a potion, and saying, "Your brother is crazy, Jack. He thinks things are chasing him. What will you do? How can you leave here now, when your brother obviously needs you? Poor darling, I'm here for you. Yes, Jack, I'll be here for you."

§

"How long have you been open?"

Selanya is pulled back to the present by the question.

"Only a few weeks."

"I'm usually downtown for openings and galas. Do you go to any of the art events in town?"

"Not very often. I would like to go to more, but the shop really keeps me busy."

Sunder looks at her cell phone as if checking the time.

"Well, it looks like a nice shop. I'll have to come back when I have more time."

She puts her cell phone into her purse and turns to leave.

"I hope to see you soon, Sunder."

Without looking back, Sunder replies, "You will."

The little bell over the door rings as Sunder goes out, and the door shuts hard behind her.

"Yeah, I'm sure I will."

Outside the door Sunder pauses for a second and rubs her amulet before she walks away.

Sunder mutters to herself, "I'm not even bothered by that weak little Jenna. She can't compete with me. But you. Well, I'm not intimidated by you either. You're just going to be more of an annoyance. Jack is mine. You need to stay away from him."

§

32

Selanya is watching through the window while Sunder walks off. As if Sunder were still in the room, Selanya replies, "You don't intimidate me either, and just so you know, I'm going to be more than an annoyance."

The Potion

After Sunder is out of sight, Selanya takes a tea kettle off of a hot plate behind the counter. She carries it on a tray with a tea box and two teacups to the sitting area in her shop. She places the tray on a table next to Shamus, who sits contemplatively in an overly fluffy chair. Selanya takes a chair near his, and she pours the hot water into their cups.

"Why have you taken such an interest in this one, Shamus?"

"Have I?"

He studies the box and carefully selects a teabag from it.

"Shamus, I've known you for a very long time now. Don't play dumb."

"I just have a feeling Jack has a more important role in the universe than he thinks he does. And this Sunder, there's something more to her too. But I'm not sure I like it."

"I know she's obsessed with him," Selanya tells him.

"Oh, there's more than that."

"What do you mean?"

"Would you like me to show you?"

"Of course."

Shamus extends his hand to her. She reaches out and lightly places her fingertips on his. She once again sees a flash of insight about Sunder.

§

Jack's brother running down a city street, he keeps looking back like someone is chasing him. Then she sees Sunder standing at a pot of simmering water, dangling a necklace over it.

"You wished you could run away. Well, you wanted to run away from all the wedding drama, but I guess I left that last part out."

Jack's brother ducks into an alley, he turns around and sees he is trapped by the thing chasing him. He is consumed by a darkness. The darkness shrinks around him and becomes a cat. Then the cat comes in a window wearing the necklace. Sunder is there waiting.

"There you are."

She takes the necklace and puts it around her neck.

"Poor Aron, you would have made a beautiful swan, but mother told me I never practiced making that potion enough.

"'Practice makes perfect,' she'd say. I guess she was right. But then where would I keep a swan in this cottage?"

§

Selanya blinks back to the present. She looks at Shamus.

"So which one of us tells him?"

Shamus looks at her with that disapproving parent glare.

"I've already told him enough. And so have you."

"But he needs to know."

"Well, at some point in time, he already does."

Selanya is about to point out that quantum physics is not a good argument in this case, but the bell above the door clatters. They both turn as they hear it.

"There's Jack now," she says as she turns back towards Shamus. But Shamus is gone. Just once she would like to see him leave through a door.

She's a Witch Too

The next morning, not five minutes after Selanya flips the sign on the door to read "Open," the bell clangs and Jack comes bouncing into the room with an enthusiastic grin.

"Hey, Selanya. Ready for the next lesson?"

"Ready if you are. Oh, I think I met a friend of yours yesterday. Sunder?"

"Sunder. Yeah, we grew up together. She's a good friend of the family."

"I think she may be more than that."

"What do you mean?"

"I just think she may want to be more than a friend."

Jack tries to process what she is saying, but he doesn't quite get it. He suffers from constant infatuation himself, but has chronic cluelessness when it comes to someone being attracted to him.

"Were you really lucky when you were a kid, Jack?"

"Aron always accused me of that. I told him I was just talented and worked hard. Why?"

Selanya wonders if she is saying too much. She hates when Shamus gives her that look, but he can be overly cautious sometimes.

"Shamus doesn't want me to tell you any of this, but I think your brother might be in danger."

"I feel the same way, but what does that have to do with me being lucky, or with Sunder?"

"There are witches that grant wishes."

"Genies? Now we're doing *I Dream of Jeannie?*"

"No. Not genies. And you're sticking with the TV show analogy?"

"Been working so far?"

"Sunder uses natural herbs and potions to grant wishes. She probably helps a lot of people, but sometimes, when witches like her get mad or obsessed . . ."

Jack starts to get annoyed, and cuts her off, "Sunder is a witch?"

Jack is doubting his sanity and his recent choices. How did he get mixed up with this woman who thinks everyone is a witch? "You think Sunder is a witch? And you think Aron did something to make her mad?"

"No. I think she's obsessed."

"Obsessed? With Aron?"

"With you."

Jack gets up to leave. Selanya knows she is pushing her luck with both with Jack and Shamus, but Jack is in some kind of trouble, and she feels compelled to help him.

"Jack, wait. I know this is a lot to take in, but hear me out."

Jack sits down, leans back, and folds his arms. His head cocks to the side ever so slightly. He is ready to let her finish then walk out.

"Okay, I can't deny that something weird is happening to

me, and maybe to Aron. But Sunder? It's going to take a lot to convince me."

Selanya takes a deep breath and begins.

Not Today, Jack

Jack is anxious to share with Jenna what Selanya told him this morning, how Sunder grants wishes. He's sitting at Jenna's kitchen table, getting the same stares from her that he gave Selanya.

"Jack, we've known Sunder since we were kids. She's not a witch."

"I know, I know. But she has been acting weird since I've been in town. Thinking back on when we were growing up, it sorta makes sense."

"This Selanya woman is crazy. You need to stay away from her."

"At least Selanya is helping me. The police aren't doing anything."

"And neither is she. She just making you loony."

"Look, you didn't see him in that alley. Something has happened to Aron, and it has something to do with witches. He bought that book because he thought someone around him is a witch, and Selanya said . . ."

"Celina is—"

" Selanya."

"Celina, Selanya, whatever, I'm not listening to this witch stuff anymore. This is supposed to be my wedding day. My fiancé is gone. I can't listen to this."

She stomps out of the room.

"Jenna."

The last thing he wanted to do was upset Jenna. How could he be so stupid and inconsiderate? His intention when he came over was to be there for her. Jack gets up and paces as he thinks for a minute. He needs to help Jenna, but if Sunder is a witch, if she did something to Aron, why? That's what he needs to know.

Selanya says Sunder uses potions. And fire fights fire, right? Jack picks up a book he brought with him from the bookstore. *Potions.* He flips through the book to one that particularly interests him. Then Jack takes his phone out of his pocket. He looks at it pensively for a moment before making a call.

"Hey. Is it okay if I come over? Jenna and I just had a fight, and I need to get out of here. I just wish . . ."

He stops himself.

On the other end of the call, Sunder can hardly contain her excitement, but keeps her usual coolness.

"What do you wish, Jack? Tell me."

"Oh, it doesn't matter."

Trust

The bell over the door rings and Shamus uncharacteristically walks into Selanya's shop. He is wearing what looks like a kimono, red with black dragon designs. His hair is pulled up into a man bun. Her initial shock of seeing the outfit is replaced by the dread she feels seeing that expression that she hates.

"If I can't let you see the past, how am I going to ever trust you with the future? What did you tell him? Our boy is in way over his head."

"He needed to know that Sunder—"

"He needed to know? Or you needed to tell him?"

Selanya opens her mouth to explain further, but finds herself staring at Shamus's outfit. Sandals. She doesn't think she has ever seen Shamus wearing sandals, always boots.

He notices her distraction, "I was in the middle of dragon training."

She really wants to know if he was being trained about dragons, training dragons, or maybe being trained by one, and mainly if there really are dragons, but she knows better than to ask any of those questions if she wants to get anything else done today.

"But back to you," Shamus says, "What did you tell Jack?"

The Truth

Jack sits on Sunder's couch as she comes in with two cups of tea and sits next to him, handing him one of the cups.

"I'm so glad you came over. I know this is hard on you."

"I just don't know if I should be worried or angry."

"You know I'm here for you, Jack. Whatever you need, just ask."

Sunder's heart races a little as Jack leans in to say something.

"Do you have cream?"

She masks her disappointment well.

"I didn't know you took cream in your tea. How British."

She sets her cup on the coffee table and goes to the kitchen. He watches her until she rounds the corner.

"Just trying something new."

Jack pulls a small vial from his pocket and dumps the contents into her tea. Sunder continues the conversation from the kitchen.

"Have the police started looking yet?"

Jack swirls the cup around a bit and quickly puts it back down before Sunder returns with the cream.

"No. They said come back tomorrow."

She hands him the cream then sits back down. He watches as she picks up her cup and begins to drink.

"I'm sure he'll show up soon. I wish there was something I could do."

"I think there may be."

Again she keeps her hopefulness from her expression. As she drinks more tea, she starts to become dizzy. She looks at her cup, then at Jack. He is watching her intensely. No longer able to hide her emotions, a look of disbelief comes over her as she realizes he has somehow drugged her.

"What have you done?"

Jack sits back. He looks coolly at her.

"Just a little truth potion. You know about potions; don't you?"

Sunder struggles to remain in control. But she is more weakened by Jack's betrayal than by the potion. She looks at him with the eyes of a wounded puppy. He stares back. She sees the anger in his eyes.

"Jack."

"Now witch, let's talk about my brother."

Episode Three
Finding Aron

The Whole Truth

Sunder's head spins. It's hard to focus. She can't believe Jack has drugged her. And with what? A truth potion? He doesn't trust her? Jack pulls her attention back to the room with an angry question.

"What did you do?"

"It was an accident, Jack!"

"What have you done to Aron?"

"I was just trying to make him run away, just keep him out of sight for a little while, so you would stay long enough."

"Long enough for what?"

Sunder does not want to answer that question. Especially not truthfully. She will make someone pay for this.

"Long enough for what?"

"For you to realize you should be with me. But you made me change him."

She believes that. It was Jack that crashed through the front door and made her drop the necklace after all.

"I made you change him?"

"You startled me. I dropped the charm. It was an accident. I never meant to do something that would hurt you."

Again, the truth. She never thinks that manipulating people to get what she wants might actually be harming them in some way. After all, she loves Jack. That's something else she believes.

"Then you need to bring him back."

"I don't know how."

"Don't lie to me, witch."

"I can't; can I? You made sure of that. Who taught you this?"

She knows the answer. Selanya. Asking something you know the answer to isn't a lie after all.

"Don't change the subject. How do we get Aron back?"

"It will require the charm and the potion, but I honestly don't know how to undo it."

She takes the necklace from around her neck and timidly hands it to him.

"I'm so sorry, Jack."

He snatches it from her hand and looks her in the eye.

"You're sorry? The potion must be wearing off."

Black Swans

Jack paces in the gift section of Selanya's shop. He has the necklace in his hand.

"She swears it was an accident. Says she was just trying to scare him into hiding. She says she doesn't know how to undo whatever she did. This is crazy. Potions. Witches. This can't be happening."

"Okay, calm down. Let me get this right. Sunder told you she was using a potion to scare your brother, but she made a mistake, and he just disappeared?"

"Disappeared. Changed. She doesn't know exactly what it did to him. it wasn't part of the spell. It went wrong. She said I made her change him. Can you believe that? She said it's my fault."

Selanya tries to keep Jack focused on the spell, but she knows his emotions are a swirling pool of betrayal, anger, confusion, and fear.

"Do you know what spell she was working? Maybe we can figure out what happened."

Jack hands the necklace to Selanya. "She used this. Something about black swans, brothers, I don't know. Fractured Fairy Tales or something. And this."

He reaches in his shirt pocket and hands her a hastily folded piece of paper. Sunder's recipe, in her own handwriting. Selanya reads the potion and holds the necklace up to the light. Jack continues talking.

"It's a recipe or potion or something. I can't believe she

would do this. I've known her since we were kids. I don't know what's real anymore."

Selanya continues calmly. "Alright. This says she was using the spell from the fairy tale of the six swans. I'm not sure how she thought that would just frighten him, but we know what she was doing, and we have the charm. That's a good place to start."

"So fairy tales are real, too?"

"Not as real as the witches they were based on. Always wondered if the Grimm brothers wrote a book of potions and hid it away somewhere. You know they must have found all sorts of information while they were collecting those stories."

Jack steps in front of her, almost nose to nose.

"Aron."

"What?"

"Just focus on helping Aron."

She realizes she was digressing. She easily distracts herself with tangents about the old days and people she met then. And she was always a bit infatuated with the Grimm brothers. They were like rock stars back then. But now back to Jack.

"Of course, Jack. I'm sorry. But some day I will tell you a few stories about the Grimms."

Damage Control

Sunder sits at Jenna's kitchen table wearing the face of a scolded child. She is very good at faces. Jenna has her face of compassion on. It's not a disguise. It is one she wears often with honesty.

"I'm sorry to be coming to you with my problems today of all days, but he was so mean to me."

"That's just not like Jack."

"I know. I didn't know what to do. He was accusing me of having something to do with Aron's disappearance."

"That's crazy."

"He called me a witch."

Jenna's face of compassion melts into one of anger and disgust.

"He's been talking to these people about witches. I don't know, Sunder. I think they've convinced him that everyone around him is a witch."

Exactly the direction Sunder wants to lead her. Just keep nudging.

"He kept saying something about a Celina, Selanya, something like that."

Jenna heats up at the mention of the name.

"Selanya. Yeah, I think she's the main one. I don't like her. I haven't met her, but I don't like her. I think she's the one that told him you were a witch."

"Why? Why would anyone say that about me?"

"I'm afraid they're using him for something. I don't know what, but this seems like some sort of scam to me. Taking advantage of him while he's upset about his brother missing."

This is going well for Sunder. She needs Jenna on her side. And Jenna's compassionate nature is such an easy target. Just play the victim, put some suggestions out there, and she will be a very strategic ally.

"Do you think they had something to do with that, Jenna?"

"I hadn't thought of that."

Sunder knows from the look on Jenna's face that she is taking the bait. This is too easy. It's like playing chess with a child. One more move.

"I'm so worried about Jack. And what if they've done something to Aron? What are we going to do, Jenna?"

Sweet Cravings

Selanya sits with a giant book of fairy tales, researching Sunder's spell. It is not the kind of magic Selanya does best. Curses, transformations, control: not on her to-do list. There's not much on the Internet, and not much in her books beyond the old fairy tales, which don't give lots of details on potions.

Jack has been waiting as patiently as Jack can. He is trying his best not to pace.

"Anything?"

"Nothing good. This is a little out of my league. No wonder Sunder messed it up."

"But you can undo it; right?"

"My magic is more about nature and organic things. Healing. This isn't as easy as an herbal potion. I may need some help on this one, or I may not do any better than Sunder did."

"Help from who? The crypto guy?"

Jack is not sure he is ready to meet the disappearing guy again. This witch world he has enter is weirder that anything he has ever dealt with, but the disappearing guy is at the top of Jack's strange list.

"No, I'd rather not have to tell Shamus about this until I have to. But I do have a strange craving for sweets. If I can't come up with anything by tomorrow morning, we'll go for a walk and see if we can find a sweet shop."

For Jack, this is an even more uncomfortable idea.

Make a Wish

Jenna has become more and more upset. Her fiancé is missing, his brother has gone crazy, and he is accusing their lifelong friend of being a witch. And their lifelong friend has worked Jenna up into an almost frenzy.

"So, Jenna, you mean she told Jack that Aron had been in the shop? So, she knew who Aron was all along."

"See, there's something really suspicious about this Selanya."

"Well she has certainly turned Jack against us."

"He's lost his mind. Aron is missing, and instead of helping me find him, Jack is playing Harry Potter with a bunch of crazies."

One more little nudge. Sunder uses her best frightened damsel voice. "You think they're dangerous? Do you think *we're* in danger?"

"Maybe so, but if I knew where to find Selanya, she'd be the one in danger."

Sunder contains how pleased she is with herself for pushing Jenna to this edge. Almost there.

"Jack mentioned meeting her at a bookstore. I can't remember where he said it was."

"If you think of it, you be sure to let me know. I just wish I could get my hands on her."

Sunder is very happy to hear her say that.

Seek Out an Expert

Selanya does not find anything in her books to help break the spell Aron is under. So, as planned, she and Jack go for walk before noon. They end up on a street of old homes with big front porches and manicured front gardens.

"This isn't the street I was on before."

"Doesn't matter."

"How can we find something that's not even there?"

Jack is annoyed to be on what seems like an impossible mission. One that he's not really sure he wants to be successful.

"Just keep thinking about finding your brother, and you'll feel it when we're close."

Selanya stops and looks at the building next to them.

"Like now."

Jack turns to see the place has not changed from the same older home, but it now has a sign hanging over steps to the porch that reads "The Sweet Woman's Shoppe."

Selanya and Jack look at each other, and without needing to say anything further, both start up the steps. When they enter the front door, they find the home is furnished like a normal house except the sitting room to the right has counters filled with sweets, and small tables with chairs. But no one is minding them. Jack is a little freaked out and questioning his sanity again.

"This isn't real, is it? I'm going to wake up, and it's all a dream, and I'm in a psycho ward somewhere. Time for your meds, Jack."

"It's as real as you and me, Jack."

"Oh, I haven't decided you're real yet."

Selanya looks at him and smiles.

"I'm having a hard time believing you are too. I know this is a lot to take in, but pull yourself together. We are here to get help."

Selanya looks around for the Sweet Woman, or a sign that she may have left a potion or instructions of some kind for them.

"The Sweet Woman has been making potions for a long, long time. She's a sort of specialist."

"That's it! I ate that special little cake she gave me, and I have been unconscious ever since, lying on a floor somewhere, dreaming all this."

Jack sits down at a table, closing his eyes and opening them several times. Waiting to wake up. But before he can leave the dream, the Sweet Woman comes in from the back of the house wearing the same flour-dusted apron. She walks over behind one of the display counters. Leaning on it, she smiles at Jack.

"Hello, Selanya, I see you brought our new friend."

Enemy of My Enemy

Sunder is collecting herbs from the kitchen cabinets, and talking to herself about what to do next and how she can use Jenna to make Jack forgive her.

"Oh, Jenna, you make this so easy. Now let's see . . . a little of chicory, a pinch of maca, some maté and bitter orange, and a whole lot of honey to cut the bitter."

She stops to think for a moment. Using Jenna to hurt Selanya will be easy. But how will she get Jack to forgive her?

Sunder stirs the mixture in a tea kettle. Revenge is easy. Forgiveness is another problem. But one thing at a time.

"Now, I'll just put the kettle on the stove, and invite my best friend over for some tea."

She picks up her phone and makes the call.

"Jenna, it's Sunder. I remembered now that Jack said the bookstore was on the North Shore. There can't be too many bookstores there. Maybe you could stop by here first and we'll go look for it together."

Chicken Bones

The Sweet Woman is talking to Selanya and Jack as she surveys the inventory in the display cases.

"The black swan spell is a very fragile recipe So many things could go wrong. It can be complicated even if the spell is intentional, but I'm not sure what would happen if it was cast by accident."

Jack is trying not to be distracted by the delicious looking inventory as the Sweet Woman adjusts the platters in the display cases. They look tasty, but that's not why he is here. He looks up and sees the Sweet Woman smiling at him. She hands him a small lemon tart.

"It's ok, Jack. I don't make them for decoration."

Jack takes a bite from the tart. His eyes roll back a little and he fights the urge to make an "mmm" sound.

Selanya stays on point. "Can we undo it?"

"I'm sure we can. I remember this man a few years back. He was a father and he accidentally turned his sons into ravens. The daughter changed them back by performing some simple task. Of course that was before my time, Lovie, but I have heard the story. My grandmother told me when I was just a child. You may remember it better, Selanya."

With a wink, the Sweet Woman holds up a chicken bone for Jack.

"If you lose this, I can make you another."

Jack starts to say something, but she stops him.

“Don't ask. You'll know when to use it.”

She holds the chicken bone out a little closer to Jack. He doesn't take it.

“For what?”

“It's a key. To help you complete the task you need to finish so you can find your brother.”

Jack is frustrated. This all has to be a hallucination. She steps closer with the bone. He steps back.

“A chicken bone? I'm supposed to feel all better now because you gave me a chicken bone? Unbelievable!”

Selanya chastises him. “Jack! Take it.”

“It's a chicken bone!”

The Sweet Woman smiles, trying not to laugh, and softly answers, “Take it.”

He reluctantly takes the bone. Selanya gives the Sweet Woman an apologetic look. She just laughs. Selanya takes Jack's arm and leads him towards the door. She looks back at the Sweet Woman and mouths, “Thank you.” After the door closes behind them, the Sweet Woman turns around to Shamus who now sits at one of the tables.

As he cuts into a piece of pie, he asks, “So what do you think? Think he'll be ok?”

“Well, we don't really know what the task that breaks the spell is, or how simple or hard it may be, or even if they will be able to complete it. All I can do is give them the key and hope the missing boy comes back with all his limbs intact.”

“That's true, but I meant Jack. Do you think Jack will be okay?”

"Good question. He's completely human as far as I can see; I'm not even sure how he got in here, Shamus."

"Me either, but I have a feeling we are going to find out, whether we want to or not."

Cup O' Tea

Sunder roams through her house looking for the cat.

"Here, kitty. You couldn't have gotten out again. Where are you?"

The doorbell rings. Jenna got here quickly. Stupid cat.

"Just a minute."

Sunder takes one last look around the room then heads to the front door.

"Alright, cat. Just stay hid until she leaves."

Sunder opens the door to find Jenna standing on the porch, tapping on her phone and nervously twisting her hair.

"Jenna, come on in."

Sunder doesn't wait to start into the script she has written.

"You know, I forgot all about this benefit dinner tonight. I am supposed to pick up the flower arrangements from the florist and take them over to the community center. I can't go with you. I'm so sorry."

"That's ok."

"But please, sit down for a while before you go to the bookstore, let me get you a cup of tea."

Metaphorically Physical

Selanya and Jack walk back to where the streets are lined with shops.

"What am I supposed to do with a chicken bone?"

"She said it's a key."

"To what?"

"I don't know. To a door? I don't know if it's a physical door or a metaphorical one."

Jack stops walking, "Or one with chicken bones on it?"

"Shut up about the chicken bone already," she replies as she keeps walking.

"No. Seriously. Look."

He points to the door beside them. It is a doorway to what looks like a narrow alley that has been walled off between two buildings. And it is decorated with chicken bones. They look at each other.

Jack gives the door a skeptical look. "It's that easy?"

"I don't know, Jack. We don't know what's behind the door."

"I think I do. The exit to the psycho ward. Time to wake up, Jack."

Then as if he does stuff like this every day, Jack puts the chicken bone in the creepy chicken-bone-covered lock, and the door opens just a crack. They look at each other again.

"Jack, be careful."

"It's ok. I know it's ok now. I mean, once you're ok with being insane, it's ok."

Jack opens the door to find a dark, misty room. No, "room" is not the right word. There is no evidence of walls. He enters first, using his cell phone as a light. Selanya follows. After a few steps, they see a glow in the distance. As they move closer, it appears to be a door. The light seeps around the edges from the other side making it the only feature they can discern through the darkness. Jack looks back at Selanya for confirmation, and she nods. They head for the door.

It is slightly ajar. With a deep breath Jack pushes it open. Inside is a banquet room. Tables set with glasses and plates, white tablecloths, and floral centerpieces. A buffet of food runs down the center of the room. The only things missing are the people at the tables.

A solitary man wearing a tux stands at the buffet. He is short, somewhere around four feet tall. He is busy filling a plate with the tasties on the buffet, but he pauses. Then he turns quickly to face the two new guests.

"Welcome! Please make yourself a plate."

Episode Four

Sweets

Jack and Selanya stand speechless as they take in the elaborate decorations, the decadent spread of food, and their host elegantly dressed and gracious host.

"The seared tuna is delicious."

Jack finally speaks. "No, thank you. We're just looking for someone."

The man looks around the room, then back at Jack.

"Do you see them?"

Jack looks around at the mostly vacant room. He notices not only the lack of people, but the lack of doors and windows. With a panic he turns back to look at the door they entered. Sure enough, it's gone.

"You might as well stay and have something to eat."

Jack slowly looks back at the man, and cautiously phrases his response. "No, thank you. We need to keep looking for my brother. Which way is the exit?"

Jack starts to look for a door. Selanya touches Jack's arm.

"Jack, maybe we should stay a minute."

"No, this feels wrong, like a trap. How do we get out of here?"

The man laughs. "Well, the food here is all free. But the

door will cost you.”

Jack's eyes widen.

“Cost us?”

Selanya eases her way in front of Jack, and responds calmly.

“I imagine you meet a good number of people here. If someone were to come through here, would you have knowledge of where that someone could be located? Or how we could take them home?”

“All sorts of people come and go through here, or come and don't go. I have lots of information on all of them.”

“What will it cost us?”

“Well, I like jewelry. Big fan of rings.”

Selanya looks at Jack. “The rings. You still have them with you?”

“The wedding rings? Yeah. Wait. No way! That's their wedding rings!”

“Oooo! Wedding rings. I do love wedding rings. Are they gold? Platinum? Tell me they're platinum.”

The man is suddenly standing beside them. Now that he's close, Jack notices his odd features. His skin has a faint green tint. His lips and fingernails are green, and his emerald green eyes have no pupils. Jack's first thought is *leprechaun*. But there's no such thing as leprechauns. Or witches. Or disappearing sweet shops. Or chicken-bone-doors, right? Jack stares at the man like he is a jack-a-lope, something you know is not real, but suddenly you see one, and you are just not sure anymore. It's all a dream. That's it. Just a strange dream.

Selanya snaps Jack back into the room. "Jack, you can get more rings. You have one brother."

Jack glances at Selanya. She *looks* real. He hesitantly takes the ring boxes out of his pocket, and hands them to the green man, who snaps them open and holds them up to the light.

"Oh yes, platinum. These are very nice. And opals. Brilliant!"

He pockets the rings and looks back at his guests.

"Are you sure you wouldn't like something to eat before you go?"

Sweets

Shamus and the Sweet Woman are sitting in a gazebo in the middle of a well-manicured garden with a mountain view. Shamus is enjoying another slice of her lemon meringue pie.

"I wonder if they have a chance of finding him," she ponders more to the wind than to Shamus.

"If it were anyone else, I would say their goose was cooked."

He smiles, quite pleased with his attempt at a pun. Swans, Geese. Sort of the same. She is not impressed.

"The spell was for a swan, not a goose. And she muddled that up and got a cat."

"Indeed, but you did end up finding the key was a chicken bone. That's like a goose."

"No. No it's not. But seriously, I wonder where they are

now."

"Once they went through that door, even I don't know. Apparently, Sunder's mother left her with some powerful potions. Too bad she isn't very good at making them."

"I don't know. Might be better that she isn't."

She watches as he savors the last bit of his pie, carefully preserved to contain just enough crust, filling, and meringue for the perfect bite.

"You really should try something else I make one day."

"But I love this pie."

The Bargain

Selanya maintains her diplomatic demeanor as she works to complete the bargain with the green gentleman.

"It's a very lovely invitation, the banquet looks amazing, and I hope I can take you up on it another time, but it really is very important that we find his brother; he has a fiancé waiting for him."

"A wedding. I do love weddings. Will there be dancing?"

"I am sure there will be."

"I do love dancing. And Cake? Petite fors?"

Selanya realizes he is trying to get an invitation. She is not sure what damage could be done by inviting him to the wedding, but she is certain that getting out of this banquet room and finding Aron depend on it.

"Jack, do you think Jenna has room for one more on her guest list?"

"Jenna really doesn't . . ."

Selanya punches his arm.

"Ow," Jack complains. Then realizing what she is driving at, he recovers.

"I . . . Jenna really doesn't . . . want to . . . exclude . . . anyone . . . who loves dancing. I am sure she would be . . . delighted to have you join us."

"Well then, there's the door. I will see you at the wedding."

To Selanya he adds, "But I am going to hold you to that rain check to visit here again."

He motions across the room to a solid wood door painted green.

"I am sure you will find the person you are looking for once you get to the other side. And I suppose since I am invited, I will need to think of something nice for the wedding present."

Selanya nods her head to the man. "Thank you."

A little courtesy goes a long way with leprechauns, Jack thinks.

"Come on, Jack, let's go."

Still feeling like he is in that space between dreaming and waking, Jack follows Selanya to the door. Maybe he won't even remember all this when he wakes up in the psychiatric ward.

They squint as they exit into the bright sunlight of the real world. Jack closes the door behind them and watches it for a moment. He looks away, and then with a jerk looks back, completely expecting the door to be gone.

"Hmmm. Still there. The rules of this game are so confusing."

"Jack, there are no real rules in this game."

"Just tell me, was he a leprechaun?"

"He was a mountain dwarf. There's no such things as leprechauns, Jack."

"Seriously? That's the line to cross? Leprechauns aren't real? Witches, yes. Mountain dwarfs, yes. Places that appear and disappear, yes. Leprechauns, not so much."

"Jack."

"And he's going to be at the wedding. Jenna will be thrilled. Hey, did you just make a date with a leprechaun?

"Mountain dwarf. And no."

"And I really thought that door would be gone by now. There's no rings, and no Aron. I just lost the rings to a leprecon man."

He smiles at her, pleased with his pun. She rolls her eyes.

"I think I see why Shamus likes you."

Before they start to walk away, there is a knock on the door. They look at each other for a moment as if waiting for the other to decide what to do.

Another knock.

Holding his breath, Jack opens the door slightly. Then wider. Inside is again dark and misty, but they both ease back a step when they see a shadowy figure standing inside. The figure steps forward into the light. It's Aron. Muddy, torn clothes, a couple of scrapes on his arms, but it's Aron.

Jack starts walking towards him.

"Aron, we're here. We're here to take you home."

But the mist grows thick around Jack until he can't see his brother. Selanya watches as both brothers vanish into the mist.

"Jack, come back!"

But with a wisp of wind, the mist clears enough for her to see Jack standing there, and beyond him, a cat. Then the mist surrounds Jack again. When it dissipates a second time, there is Jack and fifteen cats. Jack starts to panic.

"What just happened? Did Aron just split into a herd of

cats?"

Something about this seems familiar to Selanya. She remembers that there was more than the one legend about swans. There was a Celtic one.

"Jack, I think you have to pick the right one. You have to recognize your brother."

Jack spins around, slack-jawed, and looks at her.

"It's a herd of cats."

"Recognize him, Jack."

Jack looks back at the cats. All the same type of cat, but each is slightly different. Which one is the one from the alley? Then he spots it. All the cats are moving around, meowing, playing, jumping, acting like cats. But one cat is looking him in the eye. Not looking *at* him like cats tend to do, but right in the eye.

"Aron."

Then with a gush of wind and mist, the cats are gone, and Aron stands there, confused and disoriented. Jack catches him as he collapses.

The Right Stuff

Jenna is the one pacing now. Maybe not pacing so much as jittering around the room. She sits her teacup down on the coffee table and grabs her coat from the couch.

"I'm going down there now. She'd better hope she's not there when I get there."

Jenna starts to the door. Sunder smiles and follows her.

"Just be careful, Jenna. She may be dangerous."

Jenna turns around and breaks the anger just long enough for her eyes to tear up a little. "Thanks for your help, Sunder."

"Anytime, Jenna."

Jenna leaves in a rush. Sunder watches her hurry away for a moment, then closes the door and sits down on the couch. She picks up her cup and sips, pleased with a task completed.

And that didn't even take a potion. Just some words of encouragement, some good old adrenaline-pumping herbs, and a lot of maté.

Safe And Sound

Selanya is in the front of the store straightening some displays, more as a distraction from worry than doing anything productive. Jack comes in from the back room.

"He's resting. I think he's going to be ok."

"He doesn't remember anything?"

"He says the last thing he remembers is walking to the jeweler's."

The shop's front door opens with a force; the little bell over the door almost falls off. Jenna proceeds straight to Jack.

"Jenna," Jack starts.

Jenna doesn't wait to hear what he has to say, "I should have known you'd be here."

She looks at Selanya and then walks up to her so forcefully that Selanya leans back a little.

Looking Selanya in the eye but still talking to Jack, "So this is the witch?"

Jack walks over to put himself between them.

"Jenna, there's something I have to tell you."

She pushes him away.

"I'm tired of listening to you, and all these ideas that this witch has put into your head."

Selanya calmly interrupts, trying to help defuse Jenna. "We found Aron."

Jack puts his hand on Jenna's shoulder. She flinches but doesn't make him move it. He motions to the back room.

"He's resting in the back."

Jenna starts for the door. "Aron!"

Before she gets there, Aron comes through the doorway.

"Jenna?"

She rushes to him. They hold each other tight.

"I didn't know if you were alive or dead. I thought I had lost you."

"It's ok now. I'm back."

Then she asks the question that she is afraid of what the answer will be, "Where have you been?"

"I don't really know? I can't remember anything since I went to get the rings."

She lets go of the tight embrace but keeps him in her arms.

"Oh, Aron. You have amnesia?"

She turns her attention and anger back to Jack and Selanya, "He has amnesia, and you brought him here instead of a hospital? Have you lost your minds?"

Jack wants to explain, "Jenna, he's ok, he just . . ."

"Shut up! Come on Aron. I'm taking you to the hospital. We need to make sure you're okay."

She looks at Selanya as she walks Aron towards the front door.

"I don't know what she did to you, but I'm getting you out of here. And you, witch, better hope I don't have to come back."

As Aron leaves with Jenna, Jack starts to go after them, but Selanya grabs his arm.

"She'll calm down. Give her some time. At least he's ok. All his limbs are human."

"Yeah, he seemed okay. Wait. All his limbs are human?"

All's Well That Ends

Jenna leads Aron out of the store onto the city sidewalks, holding onto him as they walk. Jenna feels guilty for being glad it wasn't just cold feet.

"You don't remember anything that happened to you?

Aron shakes his head. But he reaches into his coat pocket and pulls out the ring boxes. He doesn't remember getting them, and certainly not that they were the wedding gift from a mountain dwarf.

"I remember these are for us."

Jenna's eyes tear up.

"We'll have to think about that later. Right now, we're going to the ER to get you checked out."

Her emotions are all banging against each other as they bounce off the walls of her insides. She's so relieved to find Aron. So scared of what is wrong with him. Still angry with Jack. Still wanting to get her hands around Selanya's throat. She has so many things swirling in her mind that she doesn't notice the moonlight hitting Aron's eyes, or his pupils as they reflect it, and flash into slits like a cat's.

§

Jack and Selanya stand at the front door of her shop.

"Thank you. I'm sorry Jenna thinks you were somehow responsible for what happened to Aron."

"It's okay, Jack. And you're welcome. I hope you're okay."

"I will be. This has been the strangest, most stressful few days in my life."

"I'm glad it ended well. I hope I will see you again now that it's over."

Jack smiles, "Well, once they reschedule everything, I will need a date to the wedding. Unless you're going with the leprechaun."

"I doubt he will show up, and I don't think the bride would like to see me there either." She pauses before she says, "Maybe we should just do dinner sometime."

Jack agrees that's a better option. And Selanya has the last word as he leaves the shop, "And he's a mountain dwarf."

§

The nurse calls Aron's name. Jenna goes with him into the examining room.

"I'm fine, Jenna. Everything is going to be okay."

"I know, but it doesn't hurt to let the doctor do some tests."

He smiles at her. She takes his hand in hers. Everything is going to be okay.

§

Sunder flips through her mother's cookbook. She finds the Blackened Swans recipe and adds a notation:

Be sure to hold on tight to the necklace

She closes the cookbook and puts it on the bookshelf in the kitchen. She thinks she will avoid cooking for a while. But Selanya will still have to pay, and she has to figure out a way to make Jack forgive her and realize how much he loves her.

§

Shamus and the Sweet Woman sit on a park bench overlooking the river. They both have linen napkins across their laps, along with silver forks and plates, each with a slice of lemon meringue pie.

"Well, Shamus, what do you think? All's well that ends well?"

Shamus looks pensive as he enjoys a bite of his pie. After a moment he looks at the Sweet Woman.

"All is well for our new friends, at the moment, but I think their story is just beginning."

The Legends Behind Witches

Seven Ravens

Witches and Legends One: A Bad Spell is based on several versions of a similar legend. Sunder uses a spell called Blackened Swan from her mother's cook book. This is based on the variations of ***The Seven Ravens,*** a German fairy tale collected by the Brothers Grimm. In The Seven Ravens, brothers were turned into birds. Other variations include *The Six Swans, The Twelve Wild Ducks, Udea and her Seven Brothers, The Wild Swans, The Twelve Brothers*, and *The Magic Swan Geese.*

A peasant had seven sons and one daughter. She was sickly. He sent his sons to get water for her, or to be baptized in the German version. In the Greek version, the water came from a healing spring. The brothers rushed and dropped the jug in the well. When they did not return, their father thought they had gone to play instead of fetching the water, and he cursed them. Unintentionally, he turned them into ravens.

When the sister was grown, she searched for her brothers. She asks for help from the sun, the moon, and the morning star. The morning star gives her a chicken bone (in the Italian) or a bat's foot (in the Greek) and tells her she will need it to save her brothers. She finds the Glass Mountain where they are. In the Greek, she opens it with the bat's foot; in the German, she has lost the bone, and chops off a finger to use as a key. Inside the mountain, a dwarf tells her that her brothers will return. She eats the brothers' food and drink, and leaves a ring from home in the last cup.

When her brothers return, she hides, and they turn into human form and ask who has been at their food. The last one finds the ring, and hopes it is their sister, in which case they are saved. She emerges, and they return home. In the Six Swans version, one of the brothers returns with a wing instead of an arm.

Tunders

The *tündérek* (fairies) are charming and beautiful young women that aid humans, and sometimes can ask three wishes from them. They use magical jewels and herbs to create spells. They are known to influence the emotions of humans. They are usually benevolent in nature.

Tunders are part of the documentation during the Hungarian witch trials. Testimony from the trials indicate some were known by name and highly respected for their talents.

Mountain Dwarfs

Witches and Legends draws from the Celtic and Slavic versions of Mountain Dwarfs. In Celtic mythology, dwarfs live in hidden places shrouded in enchantment. Their interaction with humans is often unpredictable, as they are wise tricksters, usually mischievous and playful. They love riddles and games, and often give humans whimsical challenges. Their stories are filled with humor and wit, showcasing a lighter side to the mythological spectrum. They are usually trying to teach the humans some lesson. They line where the line between the real and the magical is often blurred.

In Slavic mythology, like other cultures, dwarfs are often depicted as the custodians of the underground, and are associated with mining and the crafting of precious metals. They are also known as wise and ancient keepers of the earth's secrets, holding knowledge of the hidden treasures and mysteries beneath the surface. They are respected and even feared. They also like to teach humans through riddles or challenges, becoming a link between the known and the unknown while helping humans navigate the mysteries of the earth.

ABOUT THE AUTHOR

J. Smith Kirkland grew up in a 'haunted' house in Dallas Bay, Tennessee watching *Dark Shadows & The Outer Limits* – a spooky upbringing which explains why his stories tend to include ghosts, witches, folklore, and twisted plots and characters.

After obtaining degrees in Art and in Computers, and working for years in the computer industry, fate landed him in a role in the bizarre and bloody underground camp classic *Zombeak!* which stars a satan-possessed zombie-creating chicken. The experience opened a whole new world for him – one where he could share his own twisted tales by producing his own indie movies.

His indie movies include *Witches*, a soap-opera-style story which was shot in Dallas Bay and Chattanooga, Tennessee. The storylines in *Witches* are built around characters from the folklore of witches and Vodou.

Titles by J. Smith Kirkland

Non Fiction
- Growing Up Without WiFi

Fiction
- Witches and Legends Series
  - One: "A Bad Spell"
  - Two: "Curses and Cures"
  - Three: "Ghost Stories"
  - Four: "Dangers Of Magic"
- Skywords : The Incomplete Works Of J. Smith Kirkland
  - Contributions to the Crazy Buffet Club Collections 2017 thru 2025
- Tales of the Catalin Series
  - True Love
  - Spider
- Witch Ball
- Witching Hour